Pip Sits

Pip Sits

MARY MORGAN

Holiday House / New York

I LIKE TO READ is a registered trademark of Holiday House, Inc.

Copyright © 2017 by Mary Vanroyen
All Rights Reserved
HOLIDAY HOUSE is registered in the U.S. Patent and Trademark Office.
Printed and Bound in November 2016 at Tien Wah Press, Johor Bahru, Johor, Malaysia.
The artwork was created with watercolor, gouache and colored pencil.
www.holidayhouse.com
First Edition
1 3 5 7 9 10 8 6 4 2

Library of Congress Cataloging-in-Publication Data
Names: Morgan, Mary, author.
Title: Pip sits / Mary Morgan.
Description: First edition. | New York : Holiday House, [2017] | Series: I
like to read | Summary: Pip the porcupine sits on a nest of eggs, and when
they hatch, the chicks think Pip is their mother.
Identifiers: LCCN 2016004118 | ISBN 9780823436767 (hardcover)
Subjects: | CYAC: Porcupines—Fiction. | Ducks—Fiction. |
Animals—Infancy—Fiction. | Mother and child—Fiction.
Classification: LCC PZ7.M82533 Pi 2017 | DDC [E]—dc23 LC record available at https://lccn.loc.gov/2016004118

ISBN 978-0-8234-3778-8 (paperback)

For Olivia Rose and Mirabelle Grace

Mom sits.
Pip looks for fun.

Pip goes up.

He jumps.

He plops.

He peeks.

Pip sees Mother Duck.
"I have to go,"
says Mother Duck.
"Will you sit
on my eggs?"

Pip gets
in the nest.

Pip sits.

He hears
a tap.

He feels
a poke.

A duck comes out.

Mama!

"Mama!" it says.

Pop!

Pop!

Pop!

Pop!

All the ducks
come out.
"Mama!"
they say.

Mama

Mama

Mama

Pip loves
the ducks.
They sit.

They sleep.

Peep Peep

One peeps.

They all peep.

Peep
Peep
Peep
Peep
Peep
Peep
Peep
Peep

The ducks want to eat.

Mother Duck comes.

But the babies want Pip.

Peep

Peep

Peep

"Come!" says Mother Duck.
"Come!" says Pip.

Quack!

The ducks like water.

Hop

Hop

Plop

Plop

Flop

Pip does not.

Pip cries.
His mother comes.

Everyone is happy!

You will like these too!

Come Back, Ben by Ann Hassett and John Hassett
A *Kirkus Reviews* Best Book

Dinosaurs Don't, Dinosaurs Do by Steve Björkman
A Notable Social Studies Trade Book for Young People
An IRA/CBC Children's Choice

Fish Had a Wish by Michael Garland
A *Kirkus Reviews* Best Book
A Top 25 Children's Books list book

The Fly Flew In by David Catrow
An IRA/CBC Children's Choice
Maryland Blue Crab Young Reader Award Winner

Look! by Ted Lewin
The Correll Book Award for Excellence
in Early Childhood Informational Text

Me Too! by Valeri Gorbachev
A Bank Street Best Book of the Year

Mice on Ice by Rebecca Emberley and Ed Emberley
A Bank Street Best Children's Book of the Year
An IRA/CBC Children's Choice

Pig Has a Plan by Ethan Long
An IRA/CBC Children's Choice

See Me Dig by Paul Meisel
A *Kirkus Reviews* Best Book

See Me Run by Paul Meisel
A Theodor Seuss Geisel Award Honor Book
An ALA Notable Children's Book

You Can Do It by Betsy Lewin
A Bank Street Best Children's Book of the Year,
Outstanding Merit

See more I Like to Read® books.
Go to www.holidayhouse.com/I-Like-to-Read